REALLY SCARED STIFF

THREE CREEPY TALES

REALLY

SCARED STIFF

THREE CREEPY TALES

By Marshall Efron and Alfa-Betty Olsen

Illustrated by Linda Medley

A GOLDEN BOOK • NEW YORK

Western Publishing Company, Inc., Racine, Wisconsin 53404

The Red Sneakers

Jason was always losing things. He lost his schoolbooks. He lost his gloves. He lost two caps in a row, and that really upset his mother.

On Saturday, as Jason set off to play basketball, his mother gave him another cap.

"Whatever you do, Jason," she warned, "don't lose this one."

"I won't lose it," promised Jason. He put the cap on his head and forgot all about it.

Jason played basketball every Saturday. He wasn't a good player. He was usually the last one chosen and his team always lost, but he still loved playing basketball.

On his way to the playground, Jason kept saying over and over, "I hope I win today, I hope I win."

As he turned a corner, Jason saw a strange old man holding a pair of red sneakers in his bony hands.

"Your wish can come true," said the man in a hoarse whisper. "These are magic sneakers. With these sneakers, you can't lose."

"What will you take for them?" asked Jason.

"The cap on your head," rasped the man.

Jason knew that his mother would be mad at him. But he really wanted to win, so he traded his new cap.

The minute he got to the playground,
Jason put on the red sneakers. As soon as
he did, his old tennis shoes curled up into
two tennis balls and rolled away. Jason
tried to chase them, but the red sneakers
wouldn't let him. They ran in circles,
jumped, and turned—and there was nothing
Jason could do but go along with them.

The game started. Jason played like a pro! The sneakers were like wings on his feet.

"Go, Jason!" yelled his friends. His team won the first game, and the second game, and the third.

Pretty soon it got dark, and the other kids went home for supper.

"So long, Jason!" they called. "Great game!"

Now Jason was all alone in the playground, dribbling, leaping, and dunking the ball.

He tried to take off the sneakers. But to his horror, *the red sneakers would not come off his feet!*

The moon came out and cast an eerie
light. The sneakers danced Jason out of the
playground and down the dark and winding
streets. He found himself on the porch of a
creepy old house. The front door creaked
open, and the sneakers took him inside.
Behind him, the door slammed shut.

The red sneakers took Jason down to a dark, moldy basement. There he saw the old man with the bony hands. He was sitting on a huge throne made of living rats.

The old man was wearing a crown made of bones. On the wall behind him were children's hats—Jason's new cap was there, too!

"Welcome," whispered the man. He petted a cat that hissed and beat her furry tail back and forth. "I call my cat Fang."

He pointed to a big dog sleeping on the floor. "I call my dog Snarl." The dog woke up and snarled.

"And I'm calling *you* Dinner!" shrieked the man, pointing at Jason.

The sneakers suddenly rushed Jason into a large cage. The door slammed shut with a final *clang.*

13

Jason beat on the bars, but he could not get out. "What's going to happen to me?" he cried.

"Our master is going to eat you for dinner!" hissed Fang. "I'll get some of you, too. Snarl gets your bones."

"Let me out! Let me out!" Jason shouted, but the old man paid no attention.

Then Jason had an idea. He thought,
"The sneakers helped me win at basketball.
Maybe they will help me win now." Jason
jumped hard against the cage door and
kicked it wide open.

He pushed the surprised old man into
the cage along with Snarl and Fang and
slammed the door shut.

Jason grabbed his new cap off the wall
and ran up the stairs. Below him, he heard
the man cry out, "No, no! Down, Fang!
Down, Snarl! Someone, help me!" But Jason
ran out of the house and just kept going.

Jason ran toward home, but he couldn't stop jumping and turning.

He was tired and scared. If only he could take the sneakers off! Then he thought of a way to do it.

Jason began to run faster—even faster than the sneakers wanted to go. Soon the sneakers began to weaken. Jason scraped and slid and jumped.

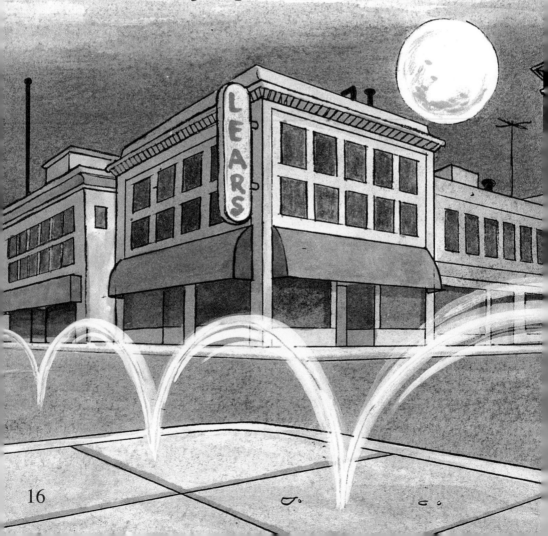

He dragged the sneakers hard against the sidewalk as he ran. The soles got thinner and thinner. Finally the red sneakers wore out and fell apart.

Jason was in charge of his own feet again! He took the tongue from one of the sneakers. He left the sneakers in the street and walked home in his socks.

17

Jason showed his cap to his mother. "See?" he said. "I didn't lose it."

"No," said his mother with a sigh, "but where are your shoes?"

"You'd never believe me," said Jason. "But I promise I'll never lose anything again."

From that day on, Jason carried the tongue of the red sneaker in his pocket—and he never lost another basketball game!

Jessica and the Ghost

The old Danvers house stood alone on a high cliff. No one had lived in it for a long, long time.

Jessica Jones and her parents were moving in. Mrs. Jones looked up at the big old house. "I wouldn't be surprised if there were secret passageways behind those walls," she said.

The next day Jessica decided to look for those secret passageways. She soon found a small dark tunnel behind a cupboard in the dining room and slipped inside. She had to crawl because the ceiling was so low.

At the end of the tunnel was a wooden door. Jessica pushed it open and found a dusty little room. The room felt spooky—as if someone were watching her. Jessica turned around and quickly crawled back to the dining room. Her heart was beating fast with fright.

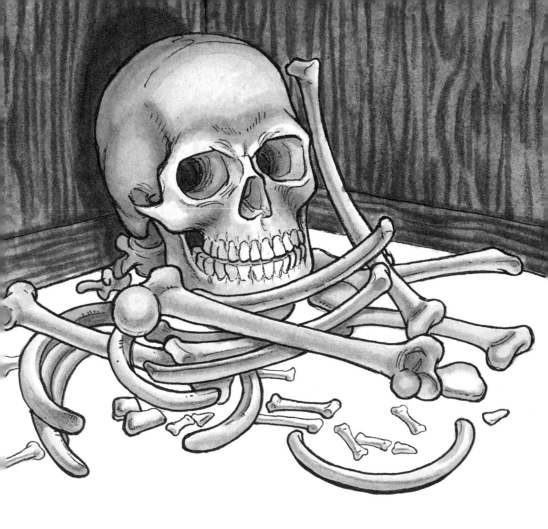

The next morning Jessica woke up feeling better. She decided to go to the secret room again. This time she found a pile of old bones and a skull in a corner. She heard a sound: *clack-clack*. The bones seemed to move. Jessica was sure someone was watching her now. She went back through the tunnel as fast as she could.

Late that same night, the door to Jessica's bedroom creaked open. Jessica woke up, afraid. "Who's there?" she called out.

"I am Captain Gore," a deep voice boomed from the doorway. There stood a ghost holding his head under his right arm. He had no left arm, and he stood on his knees because the rest of his legs were missing.

The head looked at Jessica. After a long, silent moment, it laughed a horrible laugh and drooled on the floor.

"I'll be back," said Captain Gore. Then he vanished from Jessica's room.

Jessica was still sitting up in bed when the door creaked open again and a skeleton floated into the room. Bits of flesh stuck to the skeleton's bones. A noose hung around its neck.

"I am the bloody pirate Captain Gore," said the skeleton in the same deep voice that the ghost had. "I killed and ate my victims. Then the Admiral of the Royal Navy captured me."

Captain Gore rattled his bones. "They cut off my arm and they cut off my legs, but I put up a bloody fight," he said proudly.

The skeleton's eyes glowed. "After they hanged me, they cut off my head."

"Your head is on now," said Jessica.

"Sometimes it is and sometimes it isn't. Sometimes I'm whole and sometimes I'm bones. But I'll never go away! This is *my* house!"

By now Jessica wasn't scared at all. "You're just a ghost," she said. "I've seen lots of horror movies. I know you can't hurt me."

The ghost was shocked. "What is a horror movie?" roared Captain Gore.

"We can go to one tomorrow," said Jessica. "If you're brave enough, that is."

"Captain Gore fears nothing and no one!" shouted the ghost. He rattled his bones again—and disappeared.

The next afternoon Captain Gore met
Jessica by the secret passageway. His head
was on. This time he had jet black hair,
glowing green eyes, a yellow tongue, and
gray teeth.

They walked outside and went straight to
the bus stop. No one else seemed to notice
the ghost as they boarded the bus. The bus
picked up speed. Captain Gore had never
gone so fast before. His eyes got very wide.
"This horror movie doesn't scare me!" the
ghost shouted. "Take me home."

"This isn't the horror movie," said
Jessica. "This is only the bus."

As they got off the bus, a fire engine
roared by.

"This horror movie doesn't scare me!"
screamed Captain Gore. "Take me home!"

A boy walked by with his radio playing
loud music.

"Look! That box is haunted! Take me
home!" The ghost howled and tried to run
away. Jessica had to pull him into the
movie theater.

The movie was called *The Blood Zombies Meet the Pigmen*. It was just beginning.

Captain Gore did not like the movie. He screamed "Take me home!" so loudly that everyone in the theater heard him. And now they saw him, too! Captain Gore was so frightened, he couldn't stay invisible.

An usher came down the aisle. "You'll have to keep it down," she said. "People are trying to watch the movie."

"I feel sick!" Captain Gore shouted and floated up into the air above his seat. The usher stared at him and backed away. "I'm leaving!" she yelled.

"I want to go, too," boomed Captain Gore, twirling in space.

As the ghost turned again, he saw the Pigmen on the screen. Fear made his black hair turn white. The woman sitting next to him saw it happen and fainted.

Captain Gore broke out in a cold sweat. Inside his skin, his bones began to rattle.

The man sitting behind him asked Jessica, "What's wrong with this guy?"

"Nothing much," said Jessica. "He's just a ghost."

"Weirdos," the man muttered, and he changed his seat.

Then the Blood Zombies danced with the Pigmen and became werewolves. The ghost whimpered. Jessica could see his bones shaking through his shirt.

"I don't like modern times," Captain Gore declared. "I want to leave here. I'm going. Good-bye." And with a loud *bang!*, he turned into a handful of brown dust on the seat.

Jessica swept the dust into a popcorn box. She took it home and put it in the secret room, where it gathered more dust.

Every once in a while, Jessica liked to visit the secret room. She would ask the box, "Do you want to see another horror movie, Captain Gore?"

And the box would shake!

In the Shadows

One day a traveling carnival came to Andy's town. Andy was so eager to see it, he didn't wait to go with his friends. On the very first day, he went all by himself.

Right before closing, Andy came across his favorite game—the ring toss.

A strange-looking woman was in the booth. Her left eye was green and her right eye was brown. She wore eyeglasses with no glass in them. She had red eyebrows, and her black hair stuck out around her head in spikes.

Andy paid a quarter to play the game. He lost.

The woman picked up the rings. "Say my name backward when you throw, and you might win," she said mysteriously.

"What's your name?" asked Andy.

"Lil," she said.

Andy laughed. "But Lil is the same name frontward and backward."

"I don't like it when people make fun of me," said Lil. "And just for that, I'm going to give you something you won't like."

"What is it?" asked Andy.

"You'll find out," said Lil. "But I'll tell you one thing: It's going to follow you home."

Andy had spent all his money at the carnival, so he had to walk home. He had a long way to go, and it was getting dark. The streetlights came on. The trees made long shadows on the road.

Andy remembered Lil's words: "It's going to follow you home." He looked behind him and saw his shadow. There was something strange about it.

Andy jumped to one side as fast as he could, and his shadow moved with him. That's when he saw the *other* shadow, an *extra* shadow, behind his. He recognized the hair sticking out in long spikes. It was Lil's shadow—and it was following him home!

Andy walked very fast to get away from Lil's shadow, but every time he passed a streetlight, the shadow was there. One of his feet got caught in Lil's shadow and became invisible. The foot felt very cold.

Andy tried to get his foot back. He held on to the streetlight and pulled as hard as he could. He felt as if two hands were pulling him in deeper, but he was finally able to get his foot free.

Andy ran down the dark, deserted street. The shadow came with him.

"Lil's shadow wants to get me," thought Andy. "Then my whole body will be invisible and cold."

Andy ran faster. He felt an icy chill at his back, and he ran even faster.

Andy rushed into his house and sprinted up the stairs. Lil's shadow was right behind him.

Andy made it to his room and slammed the door, but the shadow was still there.

"If I turn off the light, the shadow will go away," thought Andy. He flipped the light switch. For a minute Andy felt safe.

Then he noticed that the light of the moon was throwing shadows all over his room. He could see Lil's shadow on the floor—and it was reaching for him!

Andy tried to get away, but he wasn't fast enough. Suddenly everything went black. Andy felt colder than he'd ever felt before. He was inside Lil's shadow.

A while later Andy's mother opened the door of his room. "Andy?" she said. She turned on the light. "Andy, where are you, dear?" she asked. "Dinner is ready."

"I'm down here, on the floor, inside the shadow," Andy shouted. But his voice made no sound.

"Hmm, that's funny," Andy's mother said to herself. She flicked off the light and left. Andy's own shadow followed her out of the the room and down the stairs.

Andy's own shadow sat down at the table in Andy's place next to his little sister, Betsy. Andy's mother and father stared at it in horror. Betsy didn't seem to care. The shadow took a fork and ate Andy's dinner. Andy's mother screamed as the food disappeared into the black of the shadow.

Andy's shadow left the table and went back upstairs to Andy's room. It turned on Andy's television. Still trapped inside Lil's shadow, Andy could see his own shadow behaving like a boy.

Andy's shadow was growing more solid. Andy could see his own face appearing on the shadow's face. He could see the details of his clothing on the shadow. "Oh, no," cried Andy. "My shadow is becoming me! Soon *it* will be me and *I'll* be just a shadow."

Just then, Andy's father flung open the door and peered into his son's room.

"Andy, are you all right?" asked Andy's father. Andy's shadow turned around. In the dim light it looked exactly like Andy. "Sure, Dad," it said in Andy's voice.

"Andy, is that you?" said his father in surprise. "Your mother and I thought we saw something strange at dinner. We thought you were a . . . shadow!"

"I'm okay, Dad," said Andy's shadow.

Satisfied, his father went downstairs. Andy's shadow went to bed. And all night long the real Andy stayed trapped inside Lil's shadow.

At sunup the birds began to sing. Andy had spent a cold and sleepless night inside Lil's shadow.

Andy's shadow woke up. It now looked just like Andy. It smiled at Lil's shadow and said, "Time for us to go." It took hold of the window shade and began to pull it down.

"When the light is gone, you'll be gone," the shadow said to Andy.

Andy knew this was the end. Lil's shadow would disappear, and Andy would disappear with it.

"Oh, Lil," cried Andy, "all you wanted me to do was to say your name backward. Okay, I will—Lil. Lil! How's that?"

Andy felt a rush of air, and suddenly Lil appeared in his room. "At last, you called me," she said. She put her feet against the feet of her strange, spiky shadow. It became hers again, and Andy was free. He touched his solid arms and legs. He felt himself growing warmer.

Now Lil sent the window shade spinning to the top. Sunlight filled the room. Andy looked around and saw a new shadow stretched out behind him. His old shadow saw it, too, and screamed in fear.

"Walk to the window, Andy," said Lil.

Andy did as he was told. As he walked,
his new shadow swallowed up his old
shadow. Now his old shadow was no more.

"Say 'Thank you, Lil,'" said Lil.

"Thank you, Lil," Andy said softly.

"You're welcome, Andy," said Lil.

Then she disappeared, shadow and all,
from Andy's life.